ANDREA HEIBERG was accidentally born a few yards from Karen Blixen's home in Denmark on Hemmingway's birthday in 1955, a fortuitous beginning. Award-winning playwright and writer, her plays have been performed on Danish television and for local amateur theatre. In 2006, after walking the Camino in Spain, she had a compulsion to write her story—but in English. After almost thirty years of teaching, Heiberg moved to Sejer Island, a place that continues to inspire her love of writing.

Andrea Heiberg
Next Stop: Sejer Island

LONDON

PUBLISHED BY SALT PUBLISHING
Acre House, 11-15 William Road, London NW1 3ER,
United Kingdom

All rights reserved

© Andrea Heiberg, 2011

The right of Andrea Heiberg to be identified as the editor of
this work has been asserted by her in accordance with Section
77 of the Copyright, Designs and Patents Act 1988.

All characters and events in this publication, other than
those clearly in the public domain, are ficticious, and
any resemblance to real persons, living or dead, is purely
coincidental.

This book is in copyright. Subject to statutory exception and
to provisions of relevant collective licensing agreements, no
reproduction of any part may take place without the written
permission of Salt Publishing.

Printed and bound in Great Britain by
CPI Antony Rowe, Chippenham, Wiltshire

Typeset in Bembo 12 / 13.5

*This book is sold subject to the conditions that it shall not, by way of
trade or otherwise, be lent, re-sold, hired out, or otherwise circulated
without the publisher's prior consent in any form of binding or
cover other than that in which it is published and without a similar
condition including this condition being imposed on the subsequent
purchaser.*

ISBN 978 1 844718 70 2 paperback

1 3 5 7 9 8 6 4 2

To my niece
Mette Bodil Funder
Italy

Contents

A Kingdom for a Kalashnikov   1
Never Has There Been a Shade   10
Interpreting Golf Rule Number 25 Part B
    on Sejer Island   17
Rule Britannia   19
Where There is Fish, There is Hope   23
Solemente Para Tus Ojos   42
Numbers Never Lie   51
When Things Are Pure   69

Next Stop: Sejer Island

A Kingdom for a Kalashnikov

My house in Denmark was secured with solid wooden rods and looked like something from the Second World War. A contractor had managed to get as far as to shoring up the cellar, the entire house, with wooden rods, and he had left me with a deep hole where a toilet once was before he'd vanished with his first payment. For days I failed to reach him on multiple cell phones. I knew that he considered the work ahead of him back-breaking, but to make room for a modern bathroom the concrete floor in the cellar needed to be broken up and removed, and there'd be some serious digging to follow to lower the floor level.

'Andrea, I can do it,' Idris said the day I invited him to have a look at my cellar.

Idris is my Afghan friend from Denmark. Time and time again he had asked me for work.

'You only need to provide me with a proper drill and I'll be here Saturday,' he said.

'Saturday noon,' I said.

Saturday morning at nine sharp Idris appeared on my doorstep and just behind him someone else. I'd just stumbled out of bed.

It was early spring with rime frost outside. His friend, a thin, small man, wore no socks and just flimsy sandals. I felt as if I said good morning to Mahatma Gandhi.

'We are here for your cellar. Remember?' Idris said.

Of course I remembered. I had a heavy pneumatic drill in my car.

'We agreed "late in the morning". Late!' I emphasised.

'It is Saturday,' Idris said.

Looking at him and his friend, I didn't think this arrangement would work at all, but I felt the pressure. The new bathroom components were due in a fortnight.

Now, in the cold light of this Saturday morning, I realised I was unlikely to meet the deadline. How could I rely on these two men to break up my cellar floor? Silently, I led them both to the cellar.

'You make some coffee,' Idris said.

And I did.

A hammering began and in my dressing gown I went down to the two men, but when I opened my mouth to speak Idris said, 'Shh.'

The sandal man was now bare-footed and was on all fours, hammering here and there on the concrete floor, listening. In a few places he banged the hammer down onto the floor and then continued with a light tapping. Suddenly he rose and looked at me, almost smiling, but clearly nodding in my direction.

'This is Sedig,' Idris said. 'He is an expert.'

Sedig continued his light tapping with his tiny silver-headed hammer and I went back up to my kitchen. Half an hour later the pneumatic drill was running. The noise was infernal. Only to me it was the noise of two men working, and I liked that since I was paying them to work.

'We need more buckets,' Idris shouted.

Buckets? My neighbour had two more buckets. Idris ran in and out of the cellar door carrying buckets filled with a few pieces of concrete from the floor. This job would surely take forever. They had only removed tiny sections here and there, and Sedig alone was digging. They seemed poorly organised.

Helga, my bucket neighbour, arrived. I had already prepared an explanation about the noise, but she stopped me. 'I am here because I want to use your computer.'

The noise didn't bother her at all, she explained. 'I'm from Iceland, you know that,' she said, as if that explained anything.

The drilling continued, Helga got on-line, and I went to prepare a salad with cod and prawns when a strange deep sound, similar to the cracking of a dangerous, ice-covered sea, broke through. The noise increased and was topped with a deafening bang. I was shocked but Helga wasn't; she wasn't disturbed at all.

Down in the cellar, both Idris and Sedig were covered in dust. The entire concrete floor had turned into pebbles and was now considerably lower.

Sedig was proud, even joyful. 'Floor fixed,' he said. 'Ready for lunch now.'

Idris was merely staring, and I was too. How could he think of lunch amidst all this rubble and dust?

Back in the kitchen, I arranged my prawn salad on my grandmother's best glass crystal dishes. I was so totally distracted, and mechanically I arranged lunch to be served on antique crystal dishes for the two workmen in the cellar. So comforting it was to see the impressive tray that I added a nice cool flute of white wine.

In a few minutes Sedig gobbled up the salad. He raised the crystal dish up to the light with three fingers, and with his right hand he gave it a flick. Pling!

'Crystal,' he said to Idris.

'Beautiful crystal,' he said to me. 'Before I go to your kingdom, I go to Czechoslovakia and I make crystal glass. Good quality crystal glass and this is very good quality.'

Of course it was. It was my grandmother's.

'You went to Czechoslovakia,' I said.

'From Kabul,' he said.

'And you are a glass blower?' I said.

'Glass worker,' he corrected me and abruptly turned

to Idris as if to suggest they had spent long enough time on lunch, and Idris immediately finished his food.

They returned to digging. I left. Throughout the following hour, I heard the steady sound of their digging, a continuous rhythm. Then it stopped.

'There is something down here. It might be copper,' Idris yelled.

Helga raised her head from the computer screen. 'Copper?'

Helga and I hurried to the cellar and whatever it was, it was beautiful. A deposit of black stone ore was visible on the excavated floor of the cellar, with something in it that caught the light. Sedig was preparing to hit the stone ore in just the right place to make it crack. He tapped lightly, as if testing for the optimum place to strike.

'Wait,' Helga yelled and rushed over.

Sedig jumped up and they stood close together. She was a head taller than him. Helga is a tall, blossoming, fair-haired woman from Iceland, a Miss World-type, and she just made Sedig a Mister Old—so small and wrinkled he seemed.

He looked up at her and froze, in position.

'How extraordinary! Can I borrow your rock hammer?' Helga said.

Idris and I were reduced to being mere spectators. It was Helga's turn now to bend down and tap lightly whilst Sedig watched, and she found the exact spot she was looking for. Now she banged the hammer sharply down on the ore, and it cracked, revealing a small perfect piece of ore. She picked it up, rose and walked towards the light to inspect it more closely. Sedig followed close behind.

'It's lava stone with copper,' Helga concluded and looked down at Sedig.

'Copper stone or stone copper?' he asked.

'Lava stone with copper,' she repeated. She paused and looked down at Sedig again.

'You need some boots, otherwise your feet will get cold,' she said.

'Yes?' he said.

'You can borrow my husband's. I'll go and fetch them, but don't do anything until I get back.'

My cellar had now turned into a scientific lab with Helga in charge. Since I knew of no volcanic activity ever taking place in Denmark, I questioned this scientific line of enquiry as it might slow the work down; only there was no need to worry. The work in the cellar was nearly complete, in fact it far exceeded my expectations. So we sat waiting for Helga, drinking some more wine.

The boots were huge. Without socks, Sedig slipped into them. From looking like the Mahatma, he now looked like a clown, and Idris and I smiled. Helga had brought a tape measure as well, which she handed to Sedig, and immediately he started to uncover the ridge of the entire ore deposit. They measured together. Helga noted the results.

Helga also brought a basket with small glass jars containing lava samples and a heavy reference book for identifying varieties of lava, rocks and stones. Sedig and Helga proceeded with their investigation. They took samples and marked them. No precise match was found when compared with the lava samples in the small jars. It was not Icelandic rock. Idris and I enjoyed another bottle of wine.

Helga and Sedig carried the samples to the kitchen to have a closer look. Both Idris and I followed.

'These specimens look almost newly formed. It must have been pushed really gently along on top of the ice cap.'

'During the Ice Age?'

'Yes, it's from somewhere up north in Norway.'

'Norway?' Sedig said.

Helga looked in her stone book and pointed out pictures for Sedig who nodded.

He placed the stones in a long row and pointed at them. Idris and I had coffee.

'This is head, this is tail, this is up, and this is down,' Sedig said.

'Have you walked on a volcano?' Helga asked.

Sedig hadn't. 'I have been in Kabul, and I have seen many ores when making places to hide under Kabul.'

'You have?'

'Yes, and sometimes we must get in and out quickly, maybe in just twelve hours, and I look at the ores to find the right place to break it.'

'It's the same in Iceland,' Helga said and described the construction of a road. Her father, a building contractor, also looked for the right place when blasting through rock to make a road through the mountainous landscape.

'Of course,' Sedig laughed, 'otherwise the stones will be all over you.'

'Yes,' Helga said.

Sedig coughed. 'One day they came, all the stones, and we were caught up in a small hole. Soon no air. Soon no light. But I did like this.'

Sedig took his rock hammer and lightly tapped my kitchen wall.

'Listen,' he said, and I could hear a small difference in the sound.

'I got out,' he continued, 'but the other ones not. They were my brothers. Stones came down on them.'

'Did they suffocate or did the stones crush them?' Helga said.

'I don't know, but they were all gone. Maybe first suffocate, then squashed. The stones were just behind my back and my brothers gone. I buried my Kalashnikov and went up to the street and was free.'

We were all silent for a little while.

'Kalashnikov is not good. Everybody wants one to be a man, but it is not good. It took away our kingdom. I walk in the streets and walk on the roads, and I come to Russia. I walk again and I come to Czechoslovakia. One day I took the train to Denmark.'

'Accidents happen in Iceland, too,' Helga whispered. 'My father did not escape the last time he was blasting.He suffocated under a rock fall.'

'They fall asleep first. Deep sleep and then they sleep into death,' Sedig stressed. He explained that there was no pain. No screams.

Helga nodded again and again.

Idris and I returned to the cellar and assessed how much more work needed to be done. Idris estimated another couple of hours, and I told him it would be fine if they stopped now.

'Idris, this is just so overwhelming,' I said.

Back in the kitchen, Sedig and Helga had gone. So had all the samples. I arranged to pay for the work just in time for Sedig who came back, still wearing Helga's husband's boots. He smiled.

'No, no, no, not yet,' he said. 'There is still work to be done.'

'It's okay,' I said.

'Yes, it is. It is, today, a beautiful day!' he said, smiling cheerfully, before he disappeared back downstairs.

These two men had, in six hours, dug out and removed eight square metres of concrete and rock over two metres thick with a garden spade, a shovel and four buckets.

Never Has There Been a Shade

Dedicated to Lorena Menéndez, mezzo soprano in Buenos Aires, Argentina

IT SAYS 'SMITH' on the door. The letters carved deep in the frame in old Gothic letters, though nobody knows of any Smiths having lived here for centuries.

Nina and Frederic live in the Smith House in the centre of the village, the capital of the small island, Sejer Island. Old customs are upheld on the island, so they can't remove the door or add their names, but since no one is likely to lose their way, it doesn't matter much.

The Smith House has a proud position on its own separate hill, the medieval church occupying the next. Here history is kept alive. Due to tradition, Frederic has planted small oak trees all around the house, replacing the elms which died from disease ten years ago. He is careful not to disturb the foundation of what is thought to be the remains of a blacksmith's workshop. These oaks are almost waist high and still fighting to survive.

Frederic misses the old elms, especially on Sundays, and this Sunday morning is no exception. He stays in bed and listens to the sound of no cars, though he misses the rustling of leaves that once surrounded them. Now silence is silence, only broken by the church bell telling that the sun is up. But he needs no telling. The sun's already streaming through the window, shortening his time in bed. He's waiting for the smell of coffee, listening for the signs — Nina finishing her shower, putting the kettle on. He hears nothing, so he's still in bed.

That's when he hears a sound in the distance. The sound of an old noisy motor bike increases. The familiar sound normally announces that somebody will be receiving flowers soon. But there are no flower deliveries on Sundays. The delivery man must have got mixed up because the sound comes closer, louder and louder. The motor bike has trouble making it uphill. At any minute it could give out, but finally it succeeds. The Gold Pheasant has come to town.

Frederic is up. 'Nina!'

Noise from the kitchen reveals Nina is preparing the breakfast. 'No need to shout.'

'That imbecile has got mixed up again. How come no one ever got him a normal motor bike?'

'Wish you could be a bit more patient with him. He likes you so much.'

'He's all over me with his long stupid tales saying nothing. He's too slow, that idiot.'

The motor bike stops at the Smith House.

'Your coffee is about ready. I'll make him leave.'
Nina rushes outside.

'Fire!' the Gold Pheasant shouts. 'Now . . . fire . . . baker . . . Fred . . . help!'

The Gold Pheasant repeats this like an endless crowing. He raises his hands dramatically to the sky, pulling on his long red hair. Nobody knows why they call him the Gold Pheasant. Maybe it's this incessant pulling, or maybe it's his crimson red jacket which goes with his pepita-patterned trousers. Nobody cares. He has always looked this way.

Nina rushes inside again. 'Fred, you've got to hurry. Come down!'

The Baker House is on fire — the teacher Rasmussen's residence, which means the school is on fire. Teacher Rasmussen is running around bewildered, wearing only his white shirt and bow tie. He looks disorientated, holding a bunch of old records as if he doesn't know where to put them, staring wildly at the people arriving. Frederic is the first.

'Don't go in there,' the teacher shouts, but no one pays attention.

Frederic, along with men from the village, continues to head for the entrance, leaving teacher Rasmussen on the square in front of the house, the school yard.

The Gold Pheasant arrives. Teacher Rasmussen hasn't moved, and the Pheasant places himself right next to him, watching the spectacle. Teacher Rasmussen, a tall man, looks down studying this young man at his side.

'No school no more,' the Pheasant says.

Tears begin falling down teacher Rasmussen's cheeks. 'No school.'

'School over,' the Pheasant says.

Teacher Rasmussen wipes away his tears. 'Yes, son. School is over.'

The crackling sound is interrupted by something falling and breaking. A crowd of people yells at the entrance.

'No, school not over,' the Pheasant says. 'Now say luck!'

'Don't go!' the teacher shouts, but the Pheasant disappears in a cloud of smoke blown out from the doorway.

Village people come running, coughing, trying to carry the door. Frederic comes running, too, also coughing. He carries a three-legged chair but manages to pull Teacher Rasmussen along with him in a wild race. 'The school is coming down. Run, run!'

The roof is exploding. Everybody seeks shelter under the chestnut tree bordering the Baker House. What surprises them is the fresh air under its protecting crown.

The Gold Pheasant is nowhere to be seen.

Millions of sparks fly out from the house, and they

hear a loud crash. Having trouble breathing, no one says a word. Teacher Rasmussen sobs.

How can a three hundred-year-old building disappear this way?

Village people move to the other side of the chestnut tree, but Frederic stays with the teacher who stands like a pillar, tears streaming down his cheeks again.

'The Pheasant is in there,' the teacher says, hardly able to speak.

Frederic tries to put an arm around the teacher to move him to the others. 'The Pheasant will do fine. He's such a chicken. He just ran up to the fields.'

The teacher keeps standing, staring through the smoke. 'I don't care what you say. I want him to come back again.'

'He'll be here. He'll make it, I'm sure.'

The teacher looks down at Frederic. 'Who are you to tell? You despised that kid even though he admired you. You never knew him.'

The front walls are collapsing, blowing dust and ash right at them, sending the two of them up against the trunk of the tree. The teacher remains there, but Frederic bends down and leaps into the inferno.

The teacher shakes his head. 'This is going on forever.'

And it feels like forever before two shadows come visible through the smoke, coughing, bending down, carrying something. One of them holds a gramophone.

Frederic is pulling the Gold Pheasant who's carrying the gramophone.

The Pheasant is hardly recognizable. His long hair is gone, and both men are covered in dust, moving like two living statues, now heading for the teacher.

They stop and place the gramophone at his feet, Frederic removing the Pheasant's red jacket which covered it.

Teacher Rasmussen stands up.

'Now . . . record,' the Pheasant says.

And teacher Rasmussen looks at the Pheasant and then his records, searches, and removes one from the middle.

The Gold Pheasant takes over the remaining records. 'Now say words.'

The teacher wipes away his tears. '*Ombra mai fù!*' He clears his throat. 'Never has there been a shade of a plant more dear and lovely, or more gentle.'

The dense smoke has gone, the crackling has stopped. Small whirling clouds come up from the black ruins. Frederic turns his back to the sight and fetches the teacher's chair, the three-legged chair. People from behind the tree approach and gather around the teacher, still standing.

'Now . . . Baker song,' the Pheasant says.

The teacher puts on the record and stretches both arms up to the leaves, the tree crown. 'Ladies and gentlemen, Dame Janet Baker.'

The teacher sits down on his chair, and the Pheasant remains at his side.

And Janet Baker sings. Familiar, comforting tunes from the Baker House: '*Ombra mai fù di vegetabile, cara ed amabile, soave più.*'

A breath of fresh air from the world outside. Who doesn't touch the heavens? Here generations of children learned to love the music. Listening as they stared at the old Europe Atlas, always there, but with no Sejer Island — only for a small dot someone added with a ballpoint pen to mark its place. Today they share this song, this aria, like a national island song, though they cannot sing it. They can only listen and feel time and space, the good old days and the new ones to come.

The wives have arrived. They listen to the Baker song one more time, all together, glancing at the smoking ruins.

'Never thought I'd see my old teacher cry,' Frederic whispers to Nina.

She studies him. 'See, you cried as well.'

When the music stops, silence feels silent again.

Someone shouts, 'Look, look, we saved the door.'

Interpreting Golf Rule Number 25 Part B on Sejer Island

THE CLUB HOUSE is a former pigsty, which a certain scent reminds us of all the time. We listen to an instructor reviewing The Rule Book, his yellow shirt telling us that he's an in-comer since no real men on our island wear yellow shirts. Though I'm capable of reading, this instructor likes to read out loud every little rule. 'You're allowed to pick up your ball if it falls into a hole made by fossorial animals.'

The instructor coughs. 'What're fossorial animals, "diggers"?'

I think about dogs digging up tulips, bones —

'No, not dogs,' he says ahead of what we might say.

The third hour's just begun, proving we are extremely patient.

He nods to his audience, smiling. 'Mice are considered "diggers."'

From experience I know they're rodents.

'And water voles, newts, moles and foxes.' He carries on, describing the different holes these animals create.

Everybody's eyes rest on the local hunter who doesn't even blink. We're all expecting him to say there are no foxes on Sejer Island.

The hunter stands up. 'Guess the difference between a newt hole and a fox hole is that of a fox hole compared with one of a bear, right?'

Rule Britannia

Dedicated to poet Jacqueline Cardenas, Arizona, and poet Andrea Porter, England.

THE GREEN HILLS surround the harbour from three sides and we go up there during the summer evenings, enjoying the cooling winds and the sunset after a hot summer day. We're looking out over the old harbour watching the German and Swedish sailing boats come in for the night since Sejer Island isn't their final destination. They fly our flag, the Dannebrog, high up on top of their own in their masts, amidst many flags. They come from far out in the sea, and we smile since nobody races to be the first. As they approach, the boats pull down their sails, turn on their engines, and navigate in between the moor posts, leading them to the narrow entrance to the quay.

'Can't figure out what makes them do it,' Anna says, referring to the women who jump from the boats to the quay, loudly directed by their husbands, especially if they put the fenders to the wrong side. The husbands stay with the tillers as their wives run from one bollard to another to tie their boats. They need to be especially athletic on Sejer Island since they have to jump up onto the quay, a very dangerous manoeuvre, but these women do it all the time. Having tied up their boats, they disappear down to their cabins and the men salute each other, raising their hands to their impressive captains' hats before they secure their wives' moorings.

'Guess it's because they don't want their kitchens messed up too much,' Anna says commenting on the women's mooring activities.

These boats are like sailing caravans. The next row lines up, mooring to the first, since the quay is already occupied. Now the procedure's much more quiet and easy since no jumping is needed. Boats slowly glide in, one by one, accompanied by the noise of kitchen activities from the boats that have already arrived. From the Green Hills we smell their fried onions, wondering if they're preparing ground beef steaks for supper. The women set the tables outside on the boats, but we can't tell exactly what's served on the plates.

Our husbands join us here, eager to leave before the sun vanishes completely.

Harold, Anna's husband, glances at the sea from our position and takes out his pipe. 'There's another one out there, coming in.'

'Na, can't be,' Allan says, standing next to him.

Harold points. 'Oh, there's one all right.' And another boat approaches. 'What an amazing speed.'

Allan nods. 'Yeah, an amazing speed! Guess she's Swedish.'

'Na, she's long and slim, can't be Swedish,'

'Wonder how deep she draws?'

'She runs deep, no doubt, with those tall masts. Guess she's German.'

'She's flying. Can she be a Dutchman?' Allan says.

The question makes us smile. Both Harold and Allan are fishermen, though, and know about boats and the sea. What we know is that ships have no brakes, and this one is heading directly at our harbour at an impressive speed. A spinnaker, a huge foresail, hides what sails are up and whatever flags this vessel displays.

'She's heading for us, all right,' Harold says.

Allan nods.

The sailors below notice the boat, now, too. They're pointing as well. Some of them shout words we can't recognise.

'They needn't be scared,' Harold says. 'He's in control.'

The ferry toots from the other side of the hills, announcing its arrival back in the industry harbour. The sailors and their wives stand and face a colourful spinnaker coming right at them, listening to the loud crashing sound the huge sail releases when it comes down. Anxiety builds at the supper tables on the boats below. The approaching boat's main sail is turned, releasing another loud sound. The women remove plates, pots, and all their dishes to the cabins. The entire fleet rocks. He, the foreign sailor, heads for the mooring posts, right at them, like Danish sailors many years ago did.

'Oh, no,' Harold says. 'They're cutting their lines, and he's going for the posts.'

The German and Swedish sailors cut their mooring lines and switch on their engines. The foreign sailor throws lines round the mooring posts, one by one, like a Texas cowboy lassoing cattle. He slaloms in between the posts, followed by huge sucking sounds when he pulls the lines and turns his boat in opposite directions, then right. We watch this man and the sea, his boat. His rudder spins like a wheel. Using all our posts, he eases down the movements like the cowboy calming the calf. He avoids hitting the escaping boats, with one single wave pushing his own boat in place. He reaches the quay, and with a quick throw he fastens his boat to a bollard, then quickly to another, so it's tightened, bringing it down to 'full stop' like sailors of long ago.

We see no wife.

We're not clapping our hands, though we ought to. We stare at the boat, Union Jack emblazoned directly on its main sail. She flies no other flags, this boat, and she's called *Bear of Britain*. She's beautiful.

The captain looks up to the Green Hills and salutes, making our husbands line up and return the gesture.

'We'd better help the drifters go to the harbour,' Harold says, and the fishermen leave, heading for the industry harbour.

A woman comes forward on the English boat. She

looks up the hills and sees us. She waves. We don't know what to do.

I stand and wave back to her.

Where There is Fish, There is Hope

FROM THE FERRY, passengers follow a fishing boat as it struggles through the waves. In the row of seats by the window, they stretch to watch the light blue, wooden fishing boat bob up and down. It looks so proud, this little vessel, with its raised nose challenging the waves by going right up against them and its buoys to the rear, fixed, with red marking flags fluttering in the breeze when it heads for the bottom, having conquered yet another swell. It's a touching sight, seeing this hard-working boat on the deep blue sea, advancing.

Most of the passengers know that it won't be long before this boat will have to give in and let the bigger trawlers from the far away west coast take over its fishing rights. Time is running out for the small fishing boats, and the locals know this might be the last time they see Ernest W. Jensen out in the open steering his proud ship, *KA71*, to the jetty of Sejer Island. Ernest is the shadow in the cabin who keeps his boat steady, chugging through the waters down below the starboard deck of the towering ferry.

'Hope he's got lobsters down there,' someone says

and breaks the silence. The window passengers turn to one another. They are men returning for the weekend after a week's work in the fish factory on the mainland.

'Na, guess he's got flounders like everybody else, and they're only two a Euro.'

'He'll get paid way below two Euro for himself.'

They shake their heads.

Today, this last Friday of March, the passengers' lounge is filled with people. Fridays are always busy, but it's the first day of the summer schedule, so besides the fish factory workers, locals, and the older students, there are the tourists, the foreigners. They are easy to spot by the way they dress because the island attracts artists, but on this service one man in particular stands out. He sits motionless facing the cafeteria like any other heavy Mafioso who by accident is dropped down on this Danish ferry. He sits in the lounge with his black sunglasses, his Spanish hat, and a black leather vest, and he's watched as he waits for a woman to bring him coffee. She looks like an old hippie. What a mismatch!

Still standing and pointing with a mug of coffee, she says, 'Oh, look there. There's a fishing boat. A real old fishing boat.'

The man, motionless, says, 'Where?'

'Look to your left. It's a real cute fishing boat.'

'Oh, see this, see that,' the sunglasses man says.

The woman sits down. 'You can't see it from here. You need to stand up.'

With exaggerated difficulties, the sunglasses man gets up. He brings his mug of coffee to the windows and stands there for a while. 'Looks like a toy ship from a fair or something. Yeah, it's cute all right.' His voice is clear and strong like that of an opera singer.

'You don't need to speak so loud,' his hippie companion whispers.

'He'd better be careful that he isn't run down by the ferry.'

'Not so loud,' the woman says.

'That boat wouldn't stand a chance if it was run down by the ferry, that's all.'

The woman stands up and walks towards him. 'It's unlikely, though. Come sit with me at the table, people are staring at us.'

The ferry suddenly turns sharp northeast, now heading for the boat's course, heading to cross it. The fishing boat aims straight for the ferry for some time, but then turns.

'Oh, that bastard turned, too,' the sunglasses man says triumphantly. 'I like that. Like steering a nutshell, that's what he's doing.'

The staring fish factory workers' expressions make the sunglasses man study his vest to see if he spilt something. He finds nothing wrong, so he nods to the workers, but they've already turned their faces to the island coming up in the distance. They are looking towards home. They catch sight of the church council, lining up on the harbour wall, preparing to welcome the new pastor. They see tourists with white plastic bags, ready to buy flounders from the incoming fishing boat. They see their wives.

Anton can't help wondering what he's doing out here on Sejer Island in a priest's garden with neat paths and chestnut trees. For the moment he's listening to the chairman of the church council, a woman, describing the place, and listening to his wife's comments, peering at her once in a while as if he sees her for the very first time. He never fully understood how his wife's endless remarks and questions were instrumental in keeping up a conversation until today. The three of them are strolling around like garden enthusiasts who need the entire story, the background for this miracle that this garden, these flowers, these trees, came out of nowhere in this particular bleak spot.

'Look at this,' the chairman says and points at a bush. Anton, who is tired of being ordered to see things, looks because he promised his wife to behave and not to comment unless directly addressed. Anton's wife is Maria Magdalena Pretorius, the new pastor on Sejer.

'Couldn't you at least try to make an effort at conversation?' his wife said that morning. 'It's no big deal. Just relax and talk about the weather, flowers, birds, whatever. You don't need to see aspects of world politics in every little incident, right?'

He's *the* Anton. The jazz musician who's had to face the fact that his audience has died of old age — or, rather, most of them. The Anton, whose younger wife went to university to study theology and who has just recently, at the age of forty-eight, become a priest. She changed her name from Anne Maria to Maria Magdalena and applied for a job in the Danish Public Church. Now Anton will be the pastor's husband on Sejer Island, and he must learn to converse.

'You better get used to it,' his wife also said that morning, 'because I intend to stay here for a long time. And leave those sunglasses on the bed stand.'

This is the day the couple take formal possession of their house on the island, and that's why Anton is looking at a bush in a priest's garden, saying nothing. He sees his wife is thrilled, and she looks good in her new business dress they bought last week in Paris.

'We aren't blessed with that many herbaceous perennials, but then we have the saxifrage. We have the *Saxifraga Polyangica*, the *Saxifraga retusa*, the *Angustana* and the Cracker Jack, the *Phlox douglasii*,' the chairman says.

'What do you know,' Maria Magdalena says.

The chairman addresses Anton. 'Yeah, all those funny little names, right?'

Anton feels old.

'Yeah, great names,' he says, though he knows all about the true nature of Cracker Jacks, his favourite snack, only who's here to listen to him anyway?

'You see all the flowers in the flowerbed are violet, the colour of light. Everything means something here.

We still have the small labels your predecessor's wife put here in case you should forget the names. We only removed them to save them from the weather. You see, she worked miracles out here, changing this place so wonderfully, and we'd appreciate if you follow up her good work. Only promise us, don't touch the old roses around the entrance. They are so very old. You see, the old lady tied them back, so they appear as small rose trees.'

Lunch is inevitable. The chairman's husband joins them. He's Snoopy, the island bus driver. He only has one hour to spare, and Anton can't say he's sorry. The women do the talking. Maria Magdalena is introducing Anton, telling about his great jazz career which took him to places as far away as America, to New Orleans where he played with Miles Davis.

'Well, now that we're here,' Maria Magdalena says, 'I guess it will be too much of a change for my husband if he can't practise from time to time. Would you know of a place where he can practise?'

'I'd suggest the Seaman's Mission. I'll ask Ernest who's in charge down there. Shouldn't be a problem.'

'The Seaman's Mission,' Maria Magdalena says. 'What's that?'

'Oh, it's more of an old social club here on our island, but it doesn't play any part in peoples' lives anymore. Years ago when there were a lot of seamen there was a preacher based there, but nowadays we use the place for the children's Christmas ball and the 4th of May celebrations and stuff like that. There's a charity foundation behind it all, so they have no financial problems.'

'Only there are no seamen?'

'Yes, except for one. So it's more like a museum telling about traditions over here. For instance, all the people on the island used to write something down they wanted to be remembered and added publicly to island history. It could be a proverb, it could be anything, as long as they could see the importance of passing this personal thought on to the next generation.'

'Sounds quite interesting.'

'The inhabitants would give their sentences to the preacher, and you weren't given a second turn. There was only one chance allowed, one sentence per person. The preacher would sanction their sentences, and their words were framed so they couldn't alter them later.'

'What did you write?'

'I'm not from here, so I didn't write anything, but Snoopy's mum wrote, "Don't Knead More Dough than You Can Bake' — all the messages were put on the Wall of Pronouncements".'

'Sounds so romantic.'

'Well, not entirely. They also wrote the names of the seamen who lost their lives out there. Life back then is hard to comprehend today — risking your life for a good catch.'

'Na, but who understands death?'

'Anyway, I guess your husband can rehearse down there.'

She addresses her husband, Snoopy. 'Wouldn't you say so?'

'Yeah, shouldn't be a problem,' he says.

Snoopy is a fast eater. He finishes lunch quickly and leaves the table. He needs a pipe of tobacco.

'He can't smoke in the bus, you see, and in the priest's house we only smoke on the staircase outside,' the chairman says.

'I'm sure my husband will join him,' Maria Magdalena says, though she knows her husband avoids smoking.

For the second time Anton is in a place where he wouldn't voluntarily go. He's with this small man, the bus driver, on an old steep staircase with iron railings. He wonders if this staircase will be his to enjoy for a longer period of time, but he doesn't say anything. Instead he looks at the smoking bus driver who nods back at him.

Anton points to the roof of a barn opposite the two of them. 'I think I see a pigeon over there.'

'Yeah,' Snoopy says, big clouds of smoke swirling around his head. Anton wants a cigarette, but he must learn to forget all about them, he tells himself. He must learn to relax. He leans on the iron railing which, to his surprise, gives way under his weight, collapses, sending him tumbling down into the rose bed. He lands on his back and feels the thorns sticking in him. He finds himself entangled in rose branches and some nylon stockings the old pastor's wife used to tie up the roses.

Snoopy immediately beats his pipe against the wall on other side of the staircase, empties it, and returns to the dining room, facing Maria Magdalena.

'I think your husband ruined some of the old rose bushes,' he says. 'He fell down the stairs. He might need some help.'

Maria Magdalena could have wished for a better first day as the island's priest, something other than peeling thorns out of Anton's back, listening to his complaints. Still, he endured lunch, and all things considered, it went along fine.

Now, after the chairman couple left, she can't help laughing. 'Oh, my God, you should have seen yourself struggling with that old lady's stockings. It was all worth it.'

'All worth it? I sincerely hope so because I never played with Miles Davis. I heard him once in St. Louis. And as for New Orleans, I've never been there.'

'But it's all in the past, and no one cares who you played with and where you went. Playing jazz music in America sounds good, and I just wanted to help you get the right platform.'

She kisses his back. 'Just think, now you'll be rehearsing in the Seaman's Mission—you of all people who can't stand fish and hate the sea.'

The church is white. Dozens of layers of chalk make a thick coat, covering the Middle Age stones completely. Inside the chalk once covered all the frescos, but today they're restored under the scientific supervision of the National Museum in Copenhagen. There are pictures of Adam and Eve in chalk background. There are also the seven hills on Sejer Island with small flames above them, and there is Jesus on the white horse, returning to earth, wearing his golden crown but wearing a robe dripping with blood.

Maria Magdalena wears a black robe and a white clerical collar. From the pulpit she's seen by the congregation who wait for her first words. Anton waits, too, and so does the bishop who sits next to him.

Maria Magdalena bows, places her Bible on the small stand, and takes a good grip on the railing. 'What can I possibly say to all you good people who come here today? Last week I spent some time in Paris, and I was wondering what to say on this particular day. That's when I saw Rodin's *The Thinker*. This man who sat down because he needed to contemplate. This sculpture of a man stripped naked, internal struggles, thinking, and what would he be thinking about? Is he wondering about the meaning of his life? Rodin's sculpture doesn't reveal that, but it is worth considering: are you thinking with your mind or are you thinking with your heart? It's this philosophic question that is asked of me when I look at Rodin's Thinker, and the Bible helps us find the right answers.'

Maria Magdalena opens her Bible. She has a certain page ready. The congregation stands up.

'In the First Epistle to the Corinthians, the Apostle Paul says, "Love is patient, love is kind. It does not envy, it does not boast, it is not proud. It is not rude, it is not self-seeking, it is not easily angered, it keeps no records of wrong. Love does not delight in evil but rejoices with the truth. It always protects, always trusts, always hopes, always perseveres."'

The congregation sits down again.

'So love is the answer when we face all the changes, when there's no time to contemplate. When time is scarce, we feel alone with all the questions, and that's when we need our neighbour, because as St. Thomas Aquinas said, "Love is to will the good of another". And this is exactly what the church offers, to come here, in joining a community. There is no need to seek anymore. The Bible has the answers.'

Reading the bishop's face, Anton sees that his wife is doing fine. Recalling Rodin's Thinker, he would have said 'Thinkers' because she, his wife, demanded he see several copies of this sculpture all over Paris. He never understood the message until today when he falls in love with his wife's clear voice as if he never heard it before. The bishop is smiling.

The congregation watches them. They are eighteen loyal members of the public Danish church in the parish of Sejer—retired farmers and farm workers and retired fishermen along with their wives. Few of them hear or see well anymore, but when Snoopy's mini bus—called the church bus on Sundays—honks for them to come, they are there. They stagger toward the door and Snoopy helps them to a seat. He helps them get inside the church, and he helps them get back to their bus seats again. Safely back in the bus one by one, they begin to talk. Today they discuss who the new pastor was. Was it the man in the front row next to the bishop, or was it the woman who recited the Apostle Paul?

The voices in the bus mingle. Every passenger begins to talk without listening for an answer. Their mouths keep moving like happy little children who just learned to talk.

Unnoticed, a whining voice keeps saying, 'So much new happens all the time. It's hard to keep up with all these changes.'

It's overruled by a gruff voice who continuously says, 'Wasn't it the woman?'

'Yeah, it was the woman all right,' a shrill female voice replies.

The whiner comes through, 'She forgot the church coffee.'

'Church coffee?' a whistler says.

'There always used to be church coffee when we had a new pastor,' the whiner says.

The gruff man says, 'Someone should have mentioned that to her, and he also should have mentioned that the Apostle Paul didn't allow women to speak in churches.'

'Now you shut up. I like that bit from Paul about love and so did you once, only you've forgotten it, haven't you William E. Jensen?' the shrill woman says. 'Ages ago, you were the one who wrote the words: "Where There's Room, There is Love" down in the Seaman's Mission.'

'I never wrote that,' gruff says. 'My son wrote it.'

'No, Ernest didn't write that. You did,' the shrill woman says.

'Yeah, it was you, William. You wrote that,' the whistler says. 'And that was on the very same day when Snoopy had his saying sanctioned. Remember, Snoopy?'

Snoopy nods and smiles.

'Oh, Snoopy, that day when you showed up with that sign you took from the inn saying "No Smoking" and the preacher took it and sanctioned it,' the shrill woman says.

'Snoopy, you were far too young to come up with your message back then. It takes years to come up with the right one,' the whistler says.

'Guess you forgot the preacher added that the body is our temple, right Snoopy?' the shrill woman says.

Snoopy nods.

'In your case, Snoopy, your message should have said, "Talk is Silver, Silence is Gold",' the whiner says.

The congregation in the bus roars with laughter. They can hardly stop, but the whistler says, 'She sounded very lonely, though.'

'Of course she's lonely,' the shrill woman says. 'She has been married to a jazz musician all her life. Just like being married to a seaman where you only see him once a while and he only makes just enough money to keep you going.'

'Why didn't she just tell us about her lonely heart?'

'Because priests never do, but she'll learn, our priest, she'll learn. She's a fighter, all right. It's all there in her voice, and we have room.'

'Oh yes, "Where There is Room, There is Love".'

Snoopy smiles. He likes these rides. And he's paid extra on Sundays.

Thursday morning Anton is ready, and so is Ernest W Jensen. He wraps up two flounders from this morning's catch. He puts on his best clothes, his Sunday suit, which apart from his black suit includes a patterned vest with ivory buttons and a bow tie. He takes the flounders to the Seaman's Mission's fridge. He puts on the light in the meeting hall and adjusts a chair so all the chairs are lined up with a military precision along the long tables. He checks for dust on the oilcloths, the faded, worn oilcloths. When Anton arrives, Ernest is preparing coffee for the two of them.

Ernest shakes hands with Anton. 'I'm Ernest, and I run this place.'

He opens the fridge door, points at the packet. 'I've brought two fresh flounders for you and your misses.'

Anton bows. 'We'll be delighted, thank you.'

Ernest leads him to the meeting hall where there is a framed banner which cannot be ignored. The letters red like blood. 'Jesus shed his blood for your sake,' it says.

'Oh, don't mind that. We keep it because it's so old. My great-grandmother sewed it.'

A table is laid with two cups, plates, and cookies.

'And it was so very costly. But I guess the dye she used for the red woolen threads was worth it because there's still no sign of fading.'

Anton takes a seat.

'Sorry for the delay, but I failed to see a bus stop anywhere, and the bus driver didn't stop,' he says.

'That's because Snoopy didn't expect to pick you up. You must make an appointment the next time.'

'But he's driving up and down the island with an empty bus. How come he needs appointments?'

'I wouldn't know the answer. Guess it's his time schedule or something. Make an appointment if you need a ride with Snoopy, otherwise don't expect he sees you.'

On the wall behind Ernest there are the neatly handwritten messages, the Wall of Pronouncements. They look old, except for one. Anton sees the 'No Smoking' but returns to the new one.

'I like the "Where There is Fish, There is Hope",' he says.

'It's funny that you pick that one. I just recently wrote that and put it there. You see, it took me forty-odd years to come up with it,' Ernest says. 'All the others are older, written at least twenty years ago, way back when the preacher was still here, but back then I couldn't find the right words to my message.'

'They're so different,' Anton says and reads, '"The Chicken Came First".'

'Today we say the egg came first, right?'

Anton smiles. 'I don't know. Guess we'll never know.'

Ernest stands up and points. 'That's my father's "Where There is Room, There is Love" and over there is my grandfather's "Where There is a Son, There is Faith". Being the next in line wasn't easy, so I'm glad that I finally got it right.'

'And you did great. It's quite impressive. They all are.'

'Thanks.'

Anton takes out a CD from his bag and hands it to Ernest.

'It's my latest.'

'That's a great title — *Take The Sky*.'

'It's a line from "Summertime".'

'Summertime?'

'You don't know "Summertime"?' Anton says and

sings, 'Summertime and the living is easy. Fish are jumping and the cotton is high.'

'Na, but maybe yes because your tunes sound familiar.'

'Sorry, never was that much of a blues singer.'

Anton takes his trumpet. He goes to the centre of the room, looks around, ending up facing the 'Jesus shed his blood for your sake', concentrating, breathing. Soon he's ready with his stomach, his lungs, his cheeks, his mouth. He looks at Ernest and nods. The sound of the trumpet hits Ernest with a volume that makes him jump, but when he gets accustomed to it, he listens. The magnitude fills every corner of the Seaman's Mission. Yet, the melody is so tender. An endless simplicity, so light, is streaming, as if Anton could play forever. Anton knows, so he softens the sound before he stops. He lets it fade away. Still, Ernest can't help hearing the silence.

'You liked it?'

'I loved it. You had all our messages rattling against the wall behind me. You also filled my eyes with tears.'

'The acoustics here are great. They make it sound even better.'

Ernest shows Anton the facilities for musicians, two electric sockets. He unlocks a cupboard and shows the seamen's technical equipment, a record player and two loudspeakers. Old records in brown cardboard covers and newer ones in colourful sleeves.

'Now you've seen it all, and you're welcome whenever you want.' Ernest hands Anton the key.

They have some more coffee.

The ferry schedule says departure at 11:20 on Fridays from Sejer Island, and Maria Magdalena is beginning to worry since she and her husband are the only passengers present in the departure hall, a shed facing the harbour.

But they are the only passengers this Friday morning on the ferry. Maria Magdalena is still preparing her Sunday's sermon. Yesterday she retrieved all her predecessor's wife's flower labels, and now they are lined up on a table in the passengers' lounge.

'I like these Latin expressions. Only I don't know what *Saxifraga* means in Latin; might be someone who asks questions. But flowers asking questions?'

'It definitely has nothing to do with saxophones.'

'I knew you'd say that,' she says, 'but I like to use these names to make my sermon more relevant to Sejer Island.'

The sun breaks through the clouds.

'Now I know what I'll say. I'll say something about light, the colour violet representing the light, the knowledge. The knowledge of the saxifrage,' she says, 'and I can hint to the good old traditions in the priest's garden, and turn to the story of Adam and Eve.'

The ferry starts moving. The cafeteria hasn't opened yet, and as always, Anton sits right in front of it with his back to the windows in case he should get seasick. With fear painted all over his face, he sits staring at the offers with sausages, ketchup, mustard, hamburgers, and bread. He looks desperate.

'Oh, put on your sunglasses, will you?' his wife says.

When the cafeteria opens, she fetches two mugs of coffee. Still standing, she says, 'Look! There's Ernest in his fishing boat!'

'Where?' Anton says and jumps up.

He doesn't believe his eyes. He sees his friend, Ernest, but what concerns him is that his friend is heading for the opposite direction. Anton sees that Ernest is heading towards the west coast, where the trawlers are.

Anton recalls a news headline from last year: 'Woman Widowed by a Trawler Tragedy.' He recalls the fishing boat never stood a chance against the massive trawler.

Now Anton stares at Ernest's fishing boat going steady, chugging through the waves. He takes off his sunglasses but leaves on his Spanish hat. He rushes outside. He reaches the upper deck in seconds. He goes to the iron railings and climbs one step up, letting his knees balance his body. He lifts up both his arms, waving.

Ernest opens his cabin door and closes it immediately behind him. He looks up at Anton and waves back with both arms, too. Now he cups his hands forming a funnel to shout something Anton can't hear.

'See you, too,' Anton shouts back.

Ernest waves again and returns to his cabin, and the fishing boat continues to go straight west, chugging along.

Solemente Para Tus Ojos

LANDSCAPES, OH THOSE landscapes, curved, flat, or at best a little of both. The trees are tall, give shade, and they will always fight to remain standing. Then there are the waves. Their rising swell brings in life, but also their changing rhythms remind us that they might grow bigger, dangerous, they might even destroy. The coastline is scattered with wind-shaped bushes, stones, sandy spots with their dreams of kisses on a summer day. Only this is December, a windy December day on Sejer Island, and there's no hot sun to fear or cherish. The seven hills here form a sheltering barrier to the sea, and now they are bare and huge in their winter coats. There are no signs in the stars or in the moon to tell us the days are growing longer, so we rely on our knowledge of such things that they are. Being victims of the Siberian cold winds coming from the East, we islanders get the strangest notions, though we make it to the grocer's every day, inventing errands to have a goal. Today I need to go to the post office.

On Sejer Island we have no separate post office but a corner in the only grocer's shop to survive here. I have a letter for Maribell, which the postman delivered to me by mistake. I line up, say hello, and join a discussion of how biting cold the weather is but stay aware of moving slowly forward. We head towards a raised desk where there is no chair for the shopkeeper's wife who runs this small post office. She has a habit of resting her breasts on the counter, and no one seems to mind except me. I haven't got used to it yet, so I don't know where to look when I approach her. I hand her the letter with my eyes fixed on a spot a few inches above her head.

To my surprise, she says, 'Do us a favour! Deliver this letter for us, as there'll be no deliveries for the next two days, and it might be important. You see, Maribell doesn't get that many letters from Spain.'

'It's from Brazil,' I say. Maribell is Brazilian, so I presume it's a letter from there to my friend.

'Na, look here. That code is Spain,' the shopkeeper's wife insists, pointing at the stamp. Her heavy breasts are still resting on the counter, and that's when I notice both her hands are violet. It's as if she's wearing gloves.

'Sorry,' she says, 'I cooked beets yesterday.'

Immediately I glance up at the spot beyond her head again. Some landscapes are just too overwhelming, or maybe it's because I am unable to hear the sea.

I sit in my car in the car park, wondering what to say to Maribell. Why didn't I just take this letter to her in the first place? I just felt it was right to return it to the post office. I still do. Only I'm not sure how Maribell will see it because we don't share the same logic. For starters, I don't know where her letter box is. She and her husband don't have a door knocker or a bell, and I know I might be shouting 'Maribell' for some considerable time. The fact that they put a heavy bench right in front of their main entrance puzzles me, but Maribell says the sun shines in that spot so much. I guess she's right, but I need to prepare myself for visiting a house with no visible door. I decide to drive round to the back and go through their sheds which form a labyrinth of entrances that lead into their house, or, as in my case, more often than not, into their bathroom.

'It's a question of opening the right doors,' Maribell has said in the past, and she is right. But I'm the type of person who needs to open them all. I smile now. I have a letter to deliver, whatever the obstacles. I'll face today's problems, keeping warm, putting my emotions on standby, and dreaming of yet another day. I like to drive under the shelter of the hills. I park my car behind one of them in case I do spot a letter box where I might just put the letter.

There's no letter box. I find my way through the edges of Maribell's garden, trying to avoid trampling their bushes, and arrive in the backyard. To my relief she's there, wandering around the garden, and she's delighted to see me.

'Terrible weather for a garden tour,' I say, but she assures me every season has its beauty.

She has a funny way of pronouncing the words, and her way of speaking in basic sentences keeps me alert. I hand her the letter.

'This is a very important letter,' she says. 'I hardly dare open it.'

'From Spain?'

She nods. 'Either this is permission to dig up my mother, or it's a rejection.'

She stops to show me something in her garden. 'My baby birch trees.'

I notice that some of her sapling birch trees have somehow spread to her neighbour's garden, threatening to ruin the neat square lawn the neighbour has created with straight lines and flower beds.

'Maribell, what are your trees doing in there?'

'Oh, yeah, those trees. They're surviving. I hadn't room for them here.'

'I'm surprised your neighbour wanted them.'

'She didn't. I just put them there. You can see that they don't take up much space.'

'Oh, Maribell, you can't just plant trees in other people's gardens. That could be misunderstood.'

'She doesn't use this end of her garden, anyway, and the small trees were dying. Birches need space. They were ready to transplant, and she wasn't there, so I couldn't ask her. She should be glad to have a forest growing.'

'People with lawns don't appreciate having trees popping up in their grass,' I say and smile. I don't really know what people with lawns want, but I sense fights coming up.

'They are trees,' Maribell says, 'and she should be grateful.'

'Since she obviously likes lawns, you should move your trees again.'

'But trees can hardly grow on this island, except for this place where they are sheltered. She must learn to get used to it.'

'Oh, Maribell, sometimes I don't understand you,' I say. 'Most of all, I don't understand why you want to dig up your mother.'

'She accidentally died in Spain visiting our relatives,' she says. 'My cousins buried her, but she belongs somewhere else. That's the short version.'

'I guess the long version is that she comes from Spain?'

'Yes, but she lived in Brazil all her life, and now she's going back home there. That is if the Spanish authorities say yes.'

This comment makes trees on Sejer Island, the whole issue, fade into insignificance. What sort of person wants to transport their dead mother across oceans?

I say that I'd better go back home. It's so cold, and I'm not really dressed for it.

'You can't leave,' she says. 'I have the original Jamaican rum, the Plantation. That will melt away the cold in your bones.'

The Jamaican rum heats me up. She serves it with soda and green lemon squares and puts a wooden cocktail stick with a colourful bird in the glass.

'It's from Brazil,' she says, referring to the wooden parrot which scratches my eyeglasses when I drink.

'Yeah, it's like sitting on a Brazilian beach,' I say, though I have never set foot outside Europe.

'It is,' she says and puts on Brazilian music. Maribell likes these smooth, light tunes with men singing like women. She calls this music 'ballads for romances'.

'I'm ready for the letter now. Please stay,' she says.

The envelope is heavy. It doesn't look official, but what do I know about how things are done in Spain?

Maribell doesn't fetch a letter opener. She tears it open and manages to keep the contents on the table. There's a letter and yet another envelope inside. She takes the envelope, which doesn't seem to be addressed to anyone, and reads with wide open eyes.

'*Solemente Para tus Ojos!*'

'What's that?'

'It means "For your eyes only!" — but it has been opened. Cut open,' she says. 'Look!'

She raises it to the light but is interrupted when a picture falls out of it and lands on the floor next to me. Maribell doesn't move, so I pick it up. It's an old picture, worn, as if somebody carried it in a wallet. It's a picture of two people on a beach in bathing suits, kissing. They are wearing old-fashioned bathing suits, which tells me it's around fifty years old. I place it on the table, and Maribell stares at it.

'I never saw this picture before. It's my parents on the beach in Sao Paolo!'

'They look quite happy,' I say to say something.

'I never saw them kiss like that,' she says.

'I guess it's normal that we hide our passion from our children — but I like this picture. No doubt your parents loved each other, Maribell.'

I fear what other pictures might be in that envelope, and it's as if Maribell reads my mind. She rips open the envelope, but there are no more pictures, only a letter. Maribell reads it, her jaw dropping. She looks so shocked that I finish my drink.

'It's a letter from my father — for my mother. This is a peculiar letter. He instructs her, no, he asks her, to take his ashes to Spain to be buried with her family there. He says that he always carried the moment in his heart when he met her. That wherever he went he never saw mountains like the ones in Spain, never saw beaches that came even close to the ones back home, there, where he kissed my mother.'

'It's beautiful,' I say. 'Please translate it to me.'

Maribell isn't sure that she can read the letter out loud because it's a personal letter to her mother, but I argue that only her eyes and mine are left to read it. I tell her she should feel free to read it if she wants.

Maribell reads: 'My love, never will I forget the black mountains, never will I forget the moment when

I first saw you and needed to know your name. When I climbed those mountain slopes to reach you but only saw the sea and the sun. My darling, you raced mountains with a speed unimaginable. You said "let's go" and "let's see", and wherever you wanted to go, I'd follow. No dust, no cows, no bells ever stopped me. I only wanted to be near you. Never will I forget your father's frowned forehead when he feared his farm wouldn't be enough to feed us all. Never will I forget the beach where you wanted me to show you the world and the photographer asking how we wanted to pose for our picture. My love, on all the roads in Brazil, I always carried our photo, whatever truck I drove, our picture was always there. Landscapes, oh, landscapes, beautiful landscapes all over Brazil, that's all they are since your heart's not beating in them. So now, darling, I want you to bring me home. Get me to the black mountains where we belong. Their hearts beat for us, and the beaches below never come close to any other beaches I ever saw . . .'

I cry.

'Brazilian romances always make people cry,' Maribell says.

'Did she take him?' I say.

'You want to hear the rest of it?'

'Did she take him home?'

Maribell takes the unfolded letter from the main envelope addressed to her. Her eyes look bigger than I ever saw them before.

'She did, but then she died.'
I'm sobbing. 'Oh, it just touches me so much, sorry.'
'You need another drink?' Maribell says.
And I do.

I stumble to my car. I walked those black mountains down in Spain years ago. They, too, are my home. I, too, so many years ago, was on the beach with my husband, kissing. Only being my age, kissing on a beach is so long ago, but I do recall the images, I do recall the landscapes, and I feel my heart beating as I remember my husband's smile. There will always be landscapes, but just now I like to drive hidden by the hills on Sejer, out here, where Maribell has two huge, round hills sheltering her house. I like having a car with heated seats and that the light outside will stay for another couple of hours. Though a Dane, I have never got used to the dark days of winter. How I love that the light is winning, and I'm on my way.

I reach my home in minutes because distances on the island are short, and I don't stop to dwell on what has happened. My door closes behind me, and I'm in a world of my own, no husband anymore, long gone, a world with a letter box with my name on it and doors, two, and a bell so no one needs to call my name—but the phone is ringing. Maribell calls. She tells me she's removing her birch trees from her neighbour's lawn and she's proud because she had been toiling with the frozen soil, but managed to keep the trees alive.

'I'm putting them in the west end of our garden,' she says. 'Now you'll have to drive through the carpenter's yard, next door, to get through to me, but I'm sure he won't mind.'

Numbers Never Lie

A GREEN FIELD IS a green field, but to the sound of Walt Whitman, it will always be the playground for life and death. Most people have gone to places where they have asked themselves, *What happened here?* — not able to fully comprehend the answers, just staring at the thick layer of grass, saying a quiet prayer.

And the grass is green. It will always be so. Someone once said the grass is singing, but it takes an ear to hear it.

But the grass isn't singing on Sejer Island. Here a green field is a green field.

Bent Jensen has a green field and the question is, 'What's going on forty metres down beneath it?' It is not about what happened but what will happen the day Bent Jensen's well runs dry. When will there be no more fresh drinking water left on Sejer?

News spreads fast on the island, and being told 'don't drink the water' doesn't surprise the inhabitants; they have all watched the thick, creamy, ochre-coloured water coming out of their taps. But when the news is 'Lily's started spring cleaning,' it's different. Despite the warnings, Lily is spring cleaning.

Furniture and pictures are lined up in the garden,

oriental carpets on the washing line. Open windows, open doors. The signs are clear.

Lily believes in good old-fashioned values. The winter's soot and grease must be scrubbed away from floors, windows, walls, and ceilings, and all the curtains must be washed. She's a hard-working housewife, and she's a neighbourhood politician. She cares about her reputation, and if there is ochre in the water, so be it. No force will ever prevent her from doing her spring cleaning just before Easter.

'That's how it is,' she says. She says that concerning a lot of issues.

'I'd say she is our own little spring herald,' Frederic says to Jens.

The two men arrive at the recycling bins and Jens deposits his bags of empty red wine bottles.

'Definitely our own little spring herald,' he says, laughing. He clears his throat as both men recall the image of the stout, tall, larger-than-life Lily.

'The worst part is that my wife's got ideas as well, now,' Frederic says. 'Lily's campaign hit home, and I'm afraid I won't be able to find anything when I get back.'

'Yeah, my wife's already lining up the chairs.'

'Wives!'

The municipal administration put up two recycling bins for glass containers because of the tourists who arrive en masse during Easter. The locals need to be fast because it's well known that tourists are heavy drinkers. Frederic's car is filled with boxes of empty bottles, and like all the locals, he works quickly to get rid of the glass. Jens now leans against the car and waits for Frederic. They're headed for Half Way, the village hall just outside Sejerby, for the general meeting on the waterworks situation.

'Regin better come up with something good,' Jens says, referring to the chairman. 'Though I know that he's working day and night to get it fixed, I'm sick and tired of buying water in the store and paying waterworks bills all the same.'

'Yeah, and no one's paying me for listening to my wife's complaints,' Frederic says, 'especially when she's right. "Our water sucks, can't hardly take a shower nowadays," she says, and I promised her to do something about it, but what?'

'I promised my wife I'd do something, too.'

'Look on the bright side, I said to her one day, at least our kids don't need toothpaste, but she didn't see anything funny.'

'Yeah, we'd better do something. Our backs are to the wall.'

Frederic has finished dumping his bottles. 'What wall?'

They climb into Frederic's car, an old Volvo wagon 240, and Frederic closes his door just in time as another old Volvo 240 passes them, which makes Frederic start his and speed after it. He quickly comes to the narrow, curling road of Sejerby. They catch up with all the cars, all old Volvos, all going to Half Way, which is so named because it is half way from Sejerby to the lighthouse. Due to the short distances anywhere on the island, they soon find themselves queuing up.

'Why doesn't anybody direct traffic in the car park out there?' Frederic wonders out loud.

Jens is just about to wonder, too, when they're passed by a Volvo 260. They watch this Volvo blow down the road, its left wheels balanced on the left verge of the road. They both know that Red Prepper will probably have some long and boring excuse for driving like a mad man. Soon the line of Volvo 240s stops completely.

'Prepper never learned to park,' Frederic says.

'Oh Hell,' Jens says.

'Did you see? His car's getting rusty on the inside, too,' Frederic says.

'Na, but I saw it a few days ago.'

They can do nothing else but wait, so they sit commenting on the car in front of them, discussing the degree of decay, when a loud tapping on the right rear door almost makes Jens hit the roof. Someone is tapping on the car window with a beer bottle.

'Oh, let Fleming inside, will you?' Frederic says.

Fleming is a tall, bony man. He gets into the car with an open beer bottle in one hand and a plastic bag of beer bottles in the other. Fleming is their old schoolmate, now a sailor, who is home on leave.

'So good to be among my old buddies again,' Fleming says.

'Good to see you, too,' Frederic says but doesn't turn. He promised his wife not to hang out with Fleming, but, after all, this is just a general meeting. Both Frederic and Jens decline a beer.

They all agree that there's nothing more beautiful than a clear morning sun on Sejer Island.

At Half Way, Regin prepares the meeting. The boot of his old Toyota van is open, and he picks out things. He has his pneumatic drill, his wheelbarrow, a couple of shovels and various boxes scattered around his car, blocking the entrance to the car park. He, Regin, is the chairman, but usually he's the island blacksmith, the island handyman, so among his tools of different kinds he eventually finds the boxes that he needs today. He has asked two men to help carry his boxes of papers when Red Prepper arrives.

'Got some chicken sandwiches my wife made this morning,' Red Prepper says, and the two men follow him to get them.

'No need to hurry,' Red Prepper says, though he likes that they do.

Red Prepper describes himself as the neighbourhood politician. He likes it when all the citizens sit quietly, listening when he speaks, though the island's population of four hundred people have opinions amounting to around four hundred different political parties.

But when Prepper speaks, no one says a word. Besides being the neighbourhood politician, Red Prepper is married to the island chicken farmer who occasionally offers work and always pays well. Despite this, Prepper fails to see any connections at all between his political activities and his private life. 'It all comes down to politics,' is his favourite statement.

'Everything's under control?' he says, addressing Regin.

'Hope so,' Regin says, 'though one never knows with general meetings.'

'Those are the rules of democracy,' Prepper says. 'We never know. On the other hand, we can't deprive the citizens of speaking up, and that's what's good about Denmark. The right to speak, we must not forget freedom of speech.'

'Yeah,' Regin says and excuses himself because his cell phone rings.

In between phone calls, Regin has spent a day up at the school copying the various documents and making sure they are all there. Along with the agenda, there are letters from engineering firms, workmen of different kinds, the local water work administration department—he even has a letter from the government, attached. There's also the balance sheet, which usually causes a discussion.

Regin doesn't see the traffic jam in the parking lot, but Red Prepper stands on the staircase and wonders why people need to bring their cars when they could have so easily walked there.

'These times,' he says. 'Nothing like the good old days, and no doubt, we need changes.'

Everybody agrees as they come in.

Regin opens the general meeting. He welcomes the twelve men who found time to participate. He confirms that the meeting is legally required and the agenda is approved since no one came forward to object. The atmosphere is grave.

'I'd suggest Frederic to chair the meeting,' Regin says.

'Me?' Frederic says.

There's a short pause, but Regin applauds, which makes all those present do the same. Frederic unwillingly accepts and appoints Jens to be the secretary. The members immediately applaud again.

'Prepper has brought some of the North Field's famous chicken sandwiches,' Regin says, 'freshly made this morning.'

'Newly laid,' Frederic says, making people smile. His remark reminds them of Red Prepper's famous words reported in the local newspaper where he went out of his way to stress that his wife was the world's greatest 'egg producer.' Although this remark still makes people smile, it is, nonetheless, a fact that Red Prepper's wife produces a lot of eggs. She has 32,000 hens.

Regin continues. 'We have a bottle of Schnapps donated by our engineering firm, and our drilling firm donated a box of beer. So we're well looked after.'

People gather around the cardboard boxes containing the cellophane wrapped sandwiches and the beers while Regin pours Schnapps in small glasses that are on the tables. Gradually, member by member, they get seated.

'Let's say thanks to all our supporters,' Frederic says and instructs Jens what to write.

Jens writes and then reads: *We're legally assembled. Frederic is appointed chair, and Jens, I, appointed secretary. As announced, the meeting started at 11:00 hours, and Kirsten from North Field has again outdone herself and delivered her famous chicken sandwiches, which again this year is very much appreciated.*

'Cheers,' Frederic says and takes his beer.

'And the small glasses,' Fleming says.

'Cheers!'

Frederic notes that item number one is about 'water pressure in the pipelines' before he hands over the meeting to Regin who says 'thanks' and proceeds to deliver a tale about the expenses incurred in maintaining the old pipelines.

'As you all probably noticed, it involves a lot of digging,' Regin says and instructs the members to turn to attachment number one and not to mix it up with attachment number two which looks pretty sparse but isn't. Not according to Regin who explains that he'll comment further on that attachment later when referring to the item about the water works' account, but just now he stresses that attachment number one is a total of eleven pages. That's when a cell phone rings and a Schnapps glass falls to the floor. Regin reminds people to turn off their cell phones, and all around the table they put their phones on vibrate. He hands the bottle of Schnapps to Jens who fills up Frederic's and his own glasses before he passes it on.

'There should be useful subterranean water under Konstrup,' Regin says and holds up another piece of paper. 'Turn to attachment number two, page one, where it's clear that beneath all those layers of different soil there is a chalk layer, and as we all know, beneath chalk layers, there's fresh water.'

The people fidget with their papers.

'And this conclusion led the drilling company to commence working, and they worked for two months. Any questions?' Regin asks.

Jens can't find the conclusion in question, and it appears that one member is sitting with several copies of it while Jens has several copies of a sheet about the water pressure.

'Can I go on now?' Regin says.

'Sure,' Jens says, exchanging papers, 'we're managing fine.'

But Frederic is a bit confused and isn't sure what item he's now meant to be dealing with.

'We're dealing with item two,' Regin says. 'It's

connected to item one, but it's about the drilling results out in Konstrup.'

Fleming has a question. He asks for the Schnapps bottle.

'Can I go on?' Regin says, but his cell phone rings. 'Sorry, I forgot to turn it off.' He answers it.

The members fill up their beer glasses.

'Are you sure?' Regin says. 'No, I can't check it out. I'm at the general meeting, and you know that.'

The members follow his conversation.

'No, the harbour inspector isn't here,' Regin says, listens, and looks embarrassed. 'Why ask for him if you know he isn't here?'

A raised woman's voice cuts right through the air, and the members can't help deciphering some of the words. They all hear the end, which is, 'and you'd better go to the inn right away and do something about it. The crown prince might need a shower, you know.'

Though the caller has hung up, Regin says, 'I'll call you later.'

Frederic and Jens look at each other, smiling.

'The harbour inspector says the crown prince is here,' Regin says. 'And my wife thinks he might be heading for the inn, and they have a water situation up there.'

'What water situation?' Frederic says.

'They have no water for showering,' Regin says.

'Don't we all,' Frederic says. 'We've all got to live

with it. Nobody likes to bathe in one and a half litres of bottled water from the grocer's.'

'There's always the sea,' Fleming says.

'Wives require frequent showers,' Frederic says, addressing Fleming. 'And warm water.'

'I never recall my mum ever having a shower,' Fleming says.

Regin reminds people that the situation is serious and carries on describing the expenses related to drilling all around the island—different locations, different obstacles.

'Hold on, hold on,' Red Prepper says, tapping a teaspoon on his beer glass. 'I don't understand why we have to fill up all these test holes if that's so expensive.'

'Government regulations,' Regin says. 'We're not allowed to just leave underground bore holes, and the test holes run deep, I can tell you.'

'Numbers never lie,' Red Prepper says. 'We'll be in office after the next election. So the government may rule me here and government may rule me there—but we'll find a way round them.'

'The recycling bins you politician guys brought in are just fine. I'll give you that,' Regin says. 'But we're dealing with costs here, and I never saw your lot in the Centre Democrats eager for that sort of discussion.'

'We'll be voting for you, Prepper, we sure will,' Frederic says, which makes it obvious the assembly hasn't noticed that the Centre Democrats, as a party, disbanded some few years ago.

'What'll I write?' Jens says.

'To item number one, you write that nearly all the old pipelines have been replaced, so the pressure is fine. And to item number two, that we have secured all the test bore holes according to government regulations.'

Frederic watches Jens writing. 'No, it's not "pibelines"—it's "pipelines",' he says, and that's when all the cell phones begin to vibrate.

'Your coat's ringing,' Jens says to Frederic, though many coats are ringing, including his own.

Both men study their cell phones and decide to answer. One by one, men turn their backs to the table, bend down, and talk as low-voiced as possible, staring down at the floor.

Red Prepper stands up. 'I can't help noticing that the chairman forgets the young people,' he says, coughing. 'We in the Centre Democrats always speak up for the young people. In fact, I think we're the only ones who care. My point is, we can make the younger generation stay here if we offer them some proper work. So has the chairman considered whether young people can get some proper work digging over here?'

No one is listening, so Red Prepper coughs again and begins to repeat his speech.

'Oh, will you please be quiet?' Frederic says. 'My wife's on the phone, and it's urgent.'

'I don't know how to get water down to the inn just like that,' Regin shouts out in the room.

Red Prepper sits down.

'My wife says his majesty's still on his ship,' Jens says.

'Yes, he hasn't entered Sejer yet,' Frederic says. 'My wife suggests that we call Lily. She's got water.'

'Lily's got water?'

'Yeah, Morten's got their old well working, and with hoses we could get it to the inn.'

'We don't have hoses that long.'

'We have garden hoses.'

'Garden hoses.' Regin nods. 'Yeah, they might do the trick if we combine them all and add a pump to keep up the pressure.'

The men on the phones ask their wives to have their garden hoses ready and to ask for their neighbours' as well because all hoses will be needed.

'I'll be up at the inn in a minute,' Regin says. 'I've got to figure out how to connect it to their water system up there.'

'What if Lily says no?' Red Prepper says. 'She might do that, you know.'

'Call your wife and ask her to call Lily,' Regin says, one hand searching his pockets for car keys, the other holding his phone to his ear.

'Come to think of it, I might call Lily myself. We're both politicians, you see. Different parties, I know, but we kind of speak the same language.'

'No, have your wife call Lily.'

The Ho Chi Minh Trail is a trail far away on the

other side of the world, but it's also a path on Sejer Island. It goes from the Half Way's backyard, parallel to the road, shadowed by bushes. It doesn't go through Sejerby, but it turns sharply before the town, bordering the gardens there and leads up to the church and the inn. It continues east, but people seldom walk this way.

Frederic never imagined his wife knew of this path or knew the name the men of Sejer had given it when they used it to weave their way back from Half Way after a few drinks. He never imagined that he should be standing out here on the Ho Chi Minh Trail being in charge of garden hoses, adjusting them and having Jens connect them. Regin left them with a wheelbarrow, kits and tools. Fleming had followed with his bags of beer and now he's directing the stream of people coming in with garden hoses.

'I like to be of use,' Fleming says from time to time when leading people to the right places on the trail. 'I know the Ho Chi Minh Trail by heart.'

They reach Lily's farm in four hours, and she's waiting for them. The well, located right next to the main building, is a hole sheltered with concrete rings, and the concrete lid is off.

'Hurry up,' Lily says, 'the crown prince is on his way to the inn.'

Frederic waves the end of the hose. 'Call Regin.'

'I already did, and everything is ready. We only

need to get a man down there. I'm not having Morten do it again. He's exhausted.'

'Fleming will do it,' Frederic says.

'Me?' Fleming says. 'No way! I didn't volunteer for submarines, and the same goes for that hole. Too dangerous.'

'We'll put a rope around you,' Lily says, 'and give you a bell so we can get you back up in time.'

'I'm not gonna do it,' Fleming says.

'You don't have fatherless kids to consider,' Jens says.

'What'd you know about that?' Fleming says. 'I might have some out there.'

'Yeah, but you have no wife,' Frederic concludes.

Lily's got a rope, the bell, and a torch ready.

'Morten made a connection ready for an extension pipeline down there, so you only need to plug a piece of a hose in it.'

Fleming surrenders. Frederic hands him a piece of garden hose. Lily makes sure the rope is fastened right. Reluctantly, Fleming goes to the well with the garden hose. He places himself on the edge of it. Lily fastens the bell to the rope on his shoulder. He kneels before he lets his body go downwards, still holding on to the ridge. Lily hands him the torch.

'Let go,' Fleming says, and bit by bit, Frederic and Jens gently lower the rope and Fleming disappears. For ages they keep letting down the rope. The well is so deep that when Fleming shouts 'stop' from down below, Frederic and Jens can hardly hear him, but they stop immediately. They see the rope swinging from side to side and the glow of Fleming's torch.

'I like to see signs of life from down there,' Frederic says.

'Me, too,' Jens says.

'Don't you worry. Morten has been down there several times,' Lily says, looking at her watch. 'In two minutes it'll be time for Fleming to come up.'

That's when they hear the bell ringing. Frederic and Jens slowly pull up Fleming, both quietly praying that nothing terrible has happened. They say nothing, but both of them think the same — Fleming is heavy. When Fleming appears at the brim of the well, Lily rushes to him, pulls him out. He lies flat on the yard, breathing heavily. Lily makes him lean up against the wall of the house and carefully inspects him. Fleming looks exhausted. He's having trouble breathing. Frederic and Jens are also exhausted. They bend down on either side of him.

'Gotta get him some water,' Lily says and leaves.

She returns with a glass of water.

'I'd rather have some beer,' Fleming says.

Lily studies him. 'Guess you're fine now?'

Fleming nods. Lily's cell phone rings. It's Frederic's wife Nina on the line.

'Your wife can't reach you,' Lily says to Frederic.

'Tell her my battery is dead,' he says.

'His battery is dead,' Lily says and continues saying a number of 'oh's'.

'Can I have your water?' Frederic asks Fleming.

'Yay!' Lily shouts. 'They've got water running down in the inn now.'

She hands her cell phone to Frederic who listens and says, 'Yes, we're hungry.'

Frederic listens again, nodding. 'Yes, we're on our way home.'

But they have to wait because Lily wants to give them something. She stands there with two packages, as if she'd prepared for this moment.

'Here are the first rose potatoes from my garden, and here's a nice piece of beef to go along with it. You did a great job today, Fleming. That's how it is.'

She hands the packages to Fleming who stands up and receives them in both hands.

Lily coughs. 'Figures speak for themselves. We'll be in office after the next election, and it wouldn't do us any good if news spread that there's no water on Sejer Island, right?'

A green field is a green field. That's what Fleming sees this evening. He walked the Ho Chi Minh Trail all the way and ended up south on the island. He hears the waves and hears the birds singing. He feels relieved. Out here he finds the best spot he can and sits down with his plastic bags. The packets are gone. He gave the beef to Frederic, and Jens got the potatoes.

Now Fleming stretches his legs and feels life is wonderful. He's seen many places over the years, but never a place like this anywhere in the world. He's read Walt Whitman and loves that nothing has happened here. Bent Jensen's field is all he needs. He reaches for his plastic bags.

'That's strange,' he says to himself. He doesn't recognise the bag. He empties its contents and white sheets of papers are scattered all around him, including half a bottle of Schnapps. Fleming picks up a sheet and sees it's the drilling results from Kongstrup, the conclusion Jens was missing. Fleming sits up. He reads that Sejer Island will run out of water within the decade. Maybe tomorrow, maybe in ten years, but according to the samples from Kongstrup, Sejer Island is undoubtedly running out of water soon.

'Some news,' Fleming says to himself.

He takes another sheet and smiles when he sees it's identical to the one he just read. He picks up all the sheets, and they are all the same. Dozens of sheets saying the same thing—the water's running out.

'Not today,' Fleming says and opens the Schnapps bottle. He watches the wind take away the sheets. The conclusion with the figures, the numbers, are spreading out over Bent Jensen's field, travelling across it.

'We'll figure something out,' he says. 'We always do.'

When Things Are Pure

FREDA ISN'T DISTURBED by the many images reflected endlessly in the mirrors. She is doing her make-up, applying her foundation. She's in complete control, using her threefold make-up suitcase with drawers so she never worries about getting mixed up in the procedure. There is a space for every step performed on her face throughout the day. She starts from the first drawer on the top left and continues to the big drawers to the right, bottom. She is confident because she knows all her needs can be covered, even the four different rouges she must have, depending on what time of day it is. Now Freda is heading for the eyeliner, just finishing up her eye shadow. She turns her face back and forth, and so do all the images. She considers whether to pick the brush or the pencil, then chooses the black eyeliner pencil. She turns her head from side to side to make sure the lines are sharpened right, and she nods when she's ready for the rouge. She picks up one shade and then another, carefully studying the colours. Sunlight in Crete is a challenge. Sunlight in Heraklion, especially.

She picks a screaming red and goes gentle with the finishing powder.

'I'm ready,' she says and turns to her husband.

He looks up from his tourist magazine. With admiration he looks at her red cheeks. He looks at her, the red make-up suitcase, framed in the deep purple red velour carpet going on endlessly along with them in the mirrors. He raises his glass, nods, and finishes his whisky.

'I'll be ready in a minute,' he says, his cigarette still burning in an ashtray. His comb is in his back pocket, and that's all he needs. He does his hair. She hands him a cloth brush, and he does his shoulders as well. Proudly he offers her his arm.

The streets of Heraklion are mingling and Harold likes it this way, he says. They are filled with English tourists so the language is English. He doesn't mind this, either. He likes the cafés on Saint Catherine Square.

'Just like Venice,' Harold says.

Freda agrees.

He looks round the square. 'I like to see the cathedral is still here.'

She looks up. 'Yeah, I do, too.'

They have espresso.

'Can't wait to see Demetrius,' he says.

They are heading for Cristy's Heraklion Icons, an icon shop, the place where Demetrius sells his small pictures of religious art. A new icon will be presented, a new icon made by following a specific formula — a formula which only Demetrius knows. The icon displays Jesus holding up his right hand, and for the untrained eye there isn't much difference to spot among the different icons from various years, only Harold likes to be one of the very few who immediately finds any changes.

'No priest ever convinced me of paradise, but Demetrius almost has,' Harold says, smiling.

Freda recalls how they found the place.

'How we found the place!' Harold says. 'We can't exactly say we were looking.'

'We were looking for the bus station,' she says.

'Yeah, and Demetrius' place wasn't the shortcut I'd expected. To think of all those icons he had lined up that day. They were everywhere. All of them like saying hello.'

Back then Harold pointed at one of them, addressing Demetrius.

'Is he saying hello?'

'He is blessing you,' Demetrius said.

Harold looked at the dozen of similar icons placed side by side with a stunning accuracy.

'There's a hell of a lot of blessing going on in here, right?' Harold said.

Demetrius laughed.

'Yes, I'm a very blessed man,' he said. 'I have all I need.'

Harold looked up at the icons, moved closer to them, and studied them one by one, comparing them.

'All your icons are the same,' Harold said.

'Thank you,' Demetrius said, 'but they aren't. For a

start they come from different trees, only all trees come from the very tree.'

Harold, being the third generation of a timber company owner, listened to words which were more or less his own. 'It all comes down to the first tree.'

'The very tree,' Demetrius said, 'and I just follow the grains in the wood and let them lead me to the perfect image of love.'

'The image of love?' Harold said.

Freda had wanted their first icon. For years they returned.

'Welcome, welcome, welcome, my friends,' Demetrius says and approaches them as they enter his place. The workshop feels chilly, refreshing after the hot sun. The walls are tall and whitewashed, and just below the ceiling, the icons are displayed side by side. They are dark brown and look significant lined up on the white wall. On the counter a single icon is displayed on a small easel.

'Satisfied with your room, right?' Demetrius says.

'Just arrived, so we can't say, really.'

'Got a fine icon for you,' Demetrius says. 'He's ready to go with you.'

'We are ready for him,' Harold replies.

'He is ready,' Demetrius says, laughing, and offers them a green drink, an absinth, from a tray.

'We'll drink for the icon!'

'For Damaskinos!'

They raise their glasses with dignity in honour of the great master Michael Damaskinos, the local great icon master, and Demetrius his humble descendant keeping up the high standards of his old family tradition. Having paid respect, the couple studies the icon. 'Peace' might be a better translation—only Demetrius still claims Jesus is blessing them all.

'Got it,' Harold says.

Freda smiles. A certificate goes with the deal, and it's ready, too. The couple takes hold of the icon.

'This is the very one,' Harold says.

Demetrius wraps it up. 'Congratulations.'

Through narrow alleys the couple silently walks in line, Harold leading, carrying the icon. Like a procession they advance, their faces so grave, their backs straight. They go to their hotel room.

Harold unfolds the icon and places it facing the mirrors. 'This is the nearest to perfect we can reach.'

They spend their days in their room. Freda keeps busy trying out her newly bought make-up from the airports, and Harold likes studying his different liqueur bottles, also bought in various airports. He likes to use his hip flask and drinking set, providing Freda with small metal glasses, though she likes Martinis. Mostly he sits staring at the icon along with his drinks.

'What an extraordinary room,' he says. 'Never saw anything like it.'

On the day of departure it always takes the couple by surprise how quickly their luggage is packed. Methodically Harold searches the hotel room, but they forgot nothing. This quiet activity, though very quiet, breaks the daily routines they have built up over the past week. Freda's make-up is faint, the icon is wrapped, and their suitcases locked. They are ready to go home.

With a sudden gesture, Harold unlocks his suitcase and pulls out the hip flask and two metal glasses. 'We are making good time.'

Harold pats his fashionable suitcase. 'What man will forget anything having one of these?'

Freda nods to the door as somebody constantly knocks. A persistent hotel receptionist tells them the airplane will be delayed due to a strike by luggage staff. For how long, nobody knows, so they'll just have to wait. The airport will send busses later.

'We'll be ready,' Harold says. He knows exactly how to deal with this emergency. He reaches for a bottle of scotch.

'A bit early for this, admittedly,' he says, 'but this situation calls for something continental.'

From being the best possible hotel room they ever stayed in, they can hardly wait to get out of there now. Dressed and ready, they place themselves on the bed, leaning against the headboard, having drinks and communicating through the mirrors. Freda is upset that Harold's suitcase contains so much alcohol, but Harold comforts her. He'll get them through customs all right, but they need to stay awake. Freda explains it's not the customs worrying her.

'What if we fall asleep and miss the airplane?' she says.

Harold reassures her. He finds it interesting that he doesn't need to turn his head talking to her. 'A bit hard, though, getting used to seeing you in double.'

Freda closes her eyes. She wants to leave right away. She wants to go to the airport.

Harold focuses. 'Don't worry, love, I won't get mixed up. I promise you that we'll be the first in line.'

And they are. At one o'clock in the morning they are the first in line at the airport, waiting at the desk to sign in. Harold ran ahead with their suitcases to hold this position.

From time to time he winks to his wife. 'Soon we'll be at home, all right.'

He places the boarding passes on their pile of suitcases, letting his arm rest there, turning slightly around to smile to the man next in line behind him. The queue seems endless. Most people manage to keep up casual conversations about the delay, which makes complaints build up, leaving the queue uneasy. Forty-five minutes pass, and the voices get louder and louder, but neither Harold nor Freda take part in the arguments going on behind them. Instead their eyes are fixed at the door saying 'staff', so when a stewardess comes out and heads in their direction, Harold is ready with their boarding passes.

'It'll do us good with a nice cup of coffee and a sandwich,' he says.

'Can't wait,' Freda says.

They straighten up, turn to the desk, and they are surprised because someone, somehow, stepped ahead of them. Two sunburnt men stand right in front of them. Harold politely coughs, addresses them, but they take no notice of him. They are preoccupied, engaging each other in Swedish, having trouble balancing as they hold on to the desk. Dressed in shorts and shirts, they look like they've been dropped down here from the nearest beach. One of them wears a straw hat which he desperately tries to keep in place with his right hand, now shouting something to the stewardess.

'Don't shout at me,' she says. 'We are doing the best we can, and now you just keep quiet for a minute.'

She has a general announcement for them all. The luggage staff are still on strike, but she assures them that everything is under control. The company's cabin staff will take care of the luggage.

'Please have your boarding pass ready,' she says and turns to the Swedish men who are waving their boarding passes at her.

Everybody is ready for the procedure, and the stewardess begins. She's looking up corresponding numbers on her passenger list, but fails to find any regarding the two Swedish men. 'It's not this flight.'

The straw hat Swede points at a digital sign above the counter. 'Copenhagen,' he shouts. 'You see for yourself. It says Copenhagen and we're going to Copenhagen. It says so on our boarding pass.'

'If there's a mistake here, it's on you,' the other Swede says.

The straw hat Swede puts his suitcase on the counter. It's an artificial nappa leather suitcase, olive green, and it doesn't seem to contain anything. The stewardess though isn't distracted. She examines the passes again thoroughly and suddenly understands.

'These boarding passes are for yesterday's flight. See the dates, they are from yesterday,' she says.

The Swedes study their boarding passes.

'We missed a date, so what?' the bare-headed Swede says. 'Haven't you got room for us on this one?'

'Please step out of the line,' the stewardess says.

'I'm not stepping anywhere,' the straw hat Swede says. 'We've been sleeping under this desk the entire night to get on this plane, and you're not going to stop us.'

'I've had just about enough of this,' the stewardess says and turns to call for assistance.

'No, I've had enough of this,' the straw hat Swede says. 'I'm going home to Sweden now.'

With a sudden determination, he takes his suitcase, passes the desk, heads for the luggage shute, bends down, walks straight in there, and disappears — straw hat, nappa suitcase, and all.

Harold smiles and moves forward now. He still has the boarding passes ready and so do all the travellers in the queue behind him. Whatever anger might have built up against the airline company some minutes ago has completely vanished, and the stewardess is met with friendly smiles and kindness.

In Chania International Airport in Crete there is a metal detector gateway, a heavy metal frame which marks the border between the arrival and the departure areas. Harold is in the lead. With precision and dignity, he and Freda go through the gateway without further disruptions, and together they enter the departure hall. They are ready for the shops and restaurants, but they face a wall of glass windows reflecting the many travellers occupying rows of benches. They head for the shops, but there are none of the fashionable shops they expected to find. There are people everywhere, though. At two o'clock in the morning, everything is shuttered down, leaving around a thousand people with nothing to do. Harold and Freda give up searching for shops. They even give up searching for vacant seats.

'I think we prefer standing,' Harold says.

More flights are delayed. Just now the entire hall is waiting for the plane to Munich to be ready so more benches will become vacant. The floor is crowded with people sitting, hand luggage everywhere, and yet, a stream of people arrives, apparently from a German bus. Munich travellers. People on the floor are moving closer together to make room for the newcomers.

'We'll be standing, thank you,' Harold says every now and then to people making room on the floor.

There isn't much talking going on. Most people sit motionless, staring with empty glances at the various German tourists let in one by one. It's a welcome interruption when the alarm occasionally goes off, so when a confused German tourist makes the alarm go off again and again, it's entertaining. This German man doesn't seem to comprehend that he can't just slip through the detector without two security guards delivering him right back again. He removes his belt and watch, talking, handing his belongings to the staff who wants his wallet as well. They put it on the conveyor belt for him. He enters, but the alarm goes off again. The staff wants his shirt now, and he unbuttons, still desperately trying to engage in conversation with somebody. He must give up, though, so he passes the entrance and sets off the alarm again, only this time he jumps back. Now he is quiet. He lets go of his trousers, puts them on the conveyor belt, and he enters the departure hall in his underpants. With his mouth wide open, Harold is staring, and now he starts clapping his hands, which makes most of the other waiting passengers do the same.

'Passengers to Munich Flight 207, please go to Gate number 1.'

Hundreds of people are moving, and they squeeze

themselves into a line to be ready when Gate number 1 is opened. People on the floors reorganise themselves, and Harold makes it to a bench. Only Gate number 1 doesn't open.

'Passengers to Munich, Flight 207, please do not go to Gate number 1, but go to Gate number 3. The departure will be from Gate number 3 in a short time.'

Hundreds of people move straight across the departure hall. The Munich travellers walk over passengers' belongings, which are scattered around on the floor. They even walk over some of the passengers to make it to Gate number 3 in a hurry. Soon they are squeezing themselves in line again, impatiently waiting for the huge glass doors to open. But they don't.

'Sorry, sorry, sorry, passengers to Munich. It is gate number 1. Passengers to Munich Flight 207, please do not go to Gate number 3. The departure to Munich will be from Gate number 1 any minute.'

Immediately people on the floor move together. They look frightened, facing the same group of passengers walking all over them again. The Munich travellers are more careful this time and go crisscrossing through the hall, heading back to where they came from.

The Munich queue is nearly settled when the alarm goes off again. One single traveller, a woman, is at the gateway. She is crying behind the detector, and the staff tries to comfort her. Black mascara stripes break through the rouge down her cheeks. The alarm is turned off.

The familiar voice from the loudspeaker continues. 'Konrad Albert Müller from Munich, please go to the main entrance. I repeat, Konrad Albert Müller, please —'

The woman, framed by the detector, is still crying, even screaming from time to time.

'Konrad Albert Müller from Munich, please go to the main entrance. Your wife is waiting for you there.'

Nobody seems to be moving.

'Konrad Albert Müller, the main entrance is where the metal detector is. The alarm!'

People are looking around, Harold and Freda as well.

'Konrad Albert Müller, go to the alarm now.'

'Can't wait to see him,' Harold says.

The underpants man approaches. The mad woman looks as if she could collapse any minute, which makes the man rush through the metal detector, not taking any notice of the alarm as it goes off again. He embraces the crying woman. All the people on the floor, the benches, and at the gate are completely silent, following the spectacle. The mad woman isn't mad at all. Her husband, Konrad Albert Müller, forgot her. He left with a bus for the airport without her, but with her passport.

'Incredible' is the word people say, commenting.

'Icons,' Harold says.